ALICE'S TEA PARTY

by Lyn Calder

Illustrated by Jesse Clay

Disney
PRESS

NEW YORK

1   3   5   7   9   10   8   6   4   2

Library of Congress Cataloging-in-Publication Data
Calder, Lyn.
Alice's tea party/by Lyn Calder—1st ed.
p.   cm.
Summary: A collection of stories, recipes, games, and activities
related to having a party and based on characters and scenes in the
Walt Disney version of "Alice in Wonderland."
ISBN 1-56282-145-8 (trade)—1-56282-199-7 (lib. bdg.)
1. Children's parties—Juvenile literature.   2. Entertaining—
Juvenile literature.   [1. Parties.]   I. Title.
GV1205.C28   1992
793.2'1—dc20   91-73810   CIP   AC

"The Unbirthday Song" © 1948 The Walt Disney Music Company,
copyright renewed. Used by permission.

CONTENTS

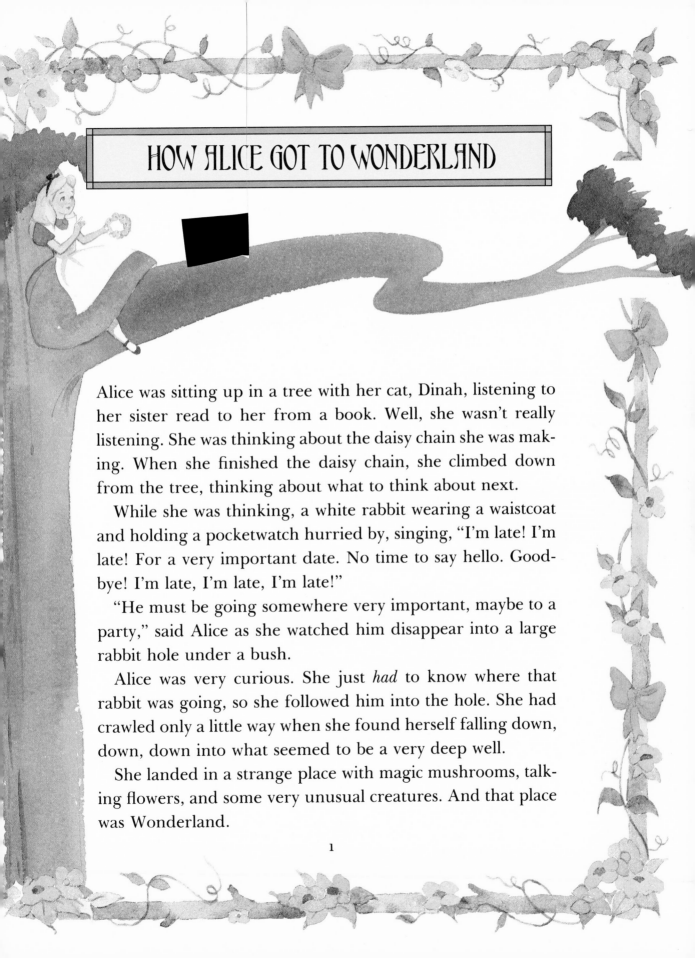

HOW ALICE GOT TO WONDERLAND

Alice was sitting up in a tree with her cat, Dinah, listening to her sister read to her from a book. Well, she wasn't really listening. She was thinking about the daisy chain she was making. When she finished the daisy chain, she climbed down from the tree, thinking about what to think about next.

While she was thinking, a white rabbit wearing a waistcoat and holding a pocketwatch hurried by, singing, "I'm late! I'm late! For a very important date. No time to say hello. Goodbye! I'm late, I'm late, I'm late!"

"He must be going somewhere very important, maybe to a party," said Alice as she watched him disappear into a large rabbit hole under a bush.

Alice was very curious. She just *had* to know where that rabbit was going, so she followed him into the hole. She had crawled only a little way when she found herself falling down, down, down into what seemed to be a very deep well.

She landed in a strange place with magic mushrooms, talking flowers, and some very unusual creatures. And that place was Wonderland.

1

THE MAD HATTER'S TEA PARTY

"I must find the White Rabbit," said Alice to herself. She made her way through Wonderland and finally came to a gate in the woods. Behind the gate was a large house with a thatched roof.

"How very curious," said Alice.

She heard strange voices singing, "A very merry unbirthday to us! To us!"

Alice stepped through the gate, and when she saw what she saw, her eyes opened wide!

There was a long, long table, set with all different kinds of teapots and cups and saucers. Nothing matched anything else. And the teapots were whistling—not the way ordinary teapots whistle when there is water boiling inside. No, these teapots

were whistling a merry tune together. And they were dancing, too!

Alice heard voices coming from the far end of the table. She saw a white-haired gentleman with a tall green hat on his head. That was the Mad Hatter.

Beside him was a floppy-eared hare in a red jacket. That was the March Hare.

Alice took a few more steps and heard them both sing, "Let's congratulate us with another cup of tea!"

Their song was so pleasant that Alice decided to sit down and listen.

I hope they offer me a cup of tea. I'm awfully thirsty, thought Alice.

"A very merry unbirthday toooo meeeee!"

As soon as the song ended, Alice began to clap and clap.

"Oh, no! No, no, no!" cried the Mad Hatter. "You can't sit there!"

"I'm so sorry. I thought it would be all right," said Alice.

"It is very rude to sit down without being invited," said the March Hare.

"I'll say it's rude!" said the Mad Hatter. "It's very, very rude."

"It's very, very, *very* rude," piped a little voice from inside a teapot. The lid popped up, and Alice saw a little gray dormouse staring straight at her.

"Why, I'm very sorry. I was enjoying the singing so much, I just wanted to get closer," said Alice.

"You enjoyed *our* singing?" said the March Hare.

4

"Oh, yes!" said Alice.

"What a delightful child!" said the Mad Hatter. "We never get compliments on our singing. You must join us for a cup of tea."

He pointed to a cup that had somehow become stuck to his elbow.

"Tea, tea. You must have a cup of tea," said the March Hare. He pulled a second cup out of the air and poured the tea with two lumps of sugar.

"That looks very nice," said Alice, reaching for the cup. "And please accept my apologies for interrupting your birthday party."

The March Hare pulled back the cup of tea before Alice could take it.

"Birthday party?" he said. "My dear child, this is not a birthday party."

"Of course it isn't," said the Mad Hatter. "This is an *un-*birthday party."

"I'm sorry, but I don't quite understand," said Alice. "What's an unbirthday?"

"It's very simple. You see, thirty days hath September. And . . . and . . . hmm. How can I explain this?" said the March Hare.

"It's easy," said the Mad Hatter. "There are 365 days in a year. If your birthday is only one day, that leaves 364 unbirthdays!"

"That means today is *my* unbirthday, too!" cried Alice.

"What a small world," said the Mad Hatter.

6

"In that case . . ." said the March Hare.

The teapots began whistling and dancing again, as the Mad Hatter and the March Hare sang their song for Alice.

"A very merry unbirthday to you!"

As they finished their song, the Mad Hatter pulled a cake out from under his hat.

"For me?" asked Alice.

"For you!" said the Mad Hatter. "Now, make a wish and blow out your candle."

Alice made her wish (she wished to find the White Rabbit, but of course she didn't say that out loud). Then she took a deep breath and blew out the candle. The cake sailed off into the sky like a rocket and—*kaboom!*—it exploded into fireworks.

7

The Dormouse must have been hiding inside the cake because he came sailing down from the starry sky, reciting a poem:

Twinkle, twinkle, little bat
How I wonder what you're at.
Up above the world you fly
Like a tea tray in the sky.

Alice clapped for the mouse. "That poem was lovely," she said.

"And now, my dear, is there any way we can help you?" asked the Mad Hatter as he dipped his saucer into his cup of tea and ate it.

"As a matter of fact, there *is* something," said Alice. "I am trying to find the White Rab—"

8

"Clean cup! Clean cup! Move down!" cried the Mad Hatter before Alice could finish her question.

"But my cup *is* clean," said Alice. "I haven't even taken a drink from it yet."

"It doesn't matter! Move down! Move down!" cried the March Hare.

The Mad Hatter and the March Hare each took Alice by the hand and moved her round the table.

"Now, would you like some more tea?" asked the Mad Hatter.

"But I haven't had any tea yet," said Alice. "So I can't very well take more."

"Ah, you mean you can't very well take less," said the March Hare.

"You can always take more than nothing," said the Mad Hatter.

The March Hare poured another cup of tea for Alice. Alice was very much looking forward to drinking it. But the Mad Hatter had put so much sugar in the cup that when Alice tried to take a sip of the tea, she got a white sugar mustache instead.

"Now, you were telling us how we can help you," said the Mad Hatter.

"Start at the very beginning," said the March Hare.

"Good idea," said the Mad Hatter. "And when you come to the end, stop."

"Well, it all started while I was with Dinah . . ." said Alice.

"Very interesting," said the March Hare. "But who is Dinah?"

"Dinah is my cat," said Alice. "You see—"

"Cat!!!" cried the Dormouse, popping up from the teapot

10

in which he was hiding. He raced around the table and burned his little nose.

"Get the jam!" cried the March Hare. "Put it on his nose!"

Alice took a spoonful of jam and spread it on the mouse's nose.

"My goodness, those are the things that upset me," said the Mad Hatter.

"See all the trouble you've started?" said the March Hare.

"I'm sorry," said Alice. "I didn't think—"

"That's the trouble," said the March Hare. "You didn't think. And when you don't think, you shouldn't talk."

He handed Alice another cup of tea. But as soon as Alice lifted the cup to her lips to drink, the Mad Hatter called, "Clean cup! Clean cup!"

11

"Move down! Move down!" called the March Hare.

They each took one of Alice's hands and moved her round the table.

"Now, continue your story," said the March Hare.

Alice was tired of moving down and tired of not getting any tea. But she still needed to know where to find the White Rabbit, so she continued her story.

"Well, I was sitting with you-know-who," said Alice, being careful not to say the word that would upset the Dormouse again.

"Wait a minute!" cried the Mad Hatter. "Who is you-know-who?"

"Oh, come now," said Alice. "You know. It's my C-A-T."

"Tea? Did you say tea?" said the Mad Hatter.

"Will half a cup be all right?" asked the March Hare. He pulled a knife from out of nowhere and cut a cup right down the middle. The Mad Hatter poured some tea into one half and somehow it stayed inside. And Alice still didn't get to drink anything because the March Hare took the cup and drank it himself.

"Don't you care for tea?" asked the March Hare.

"Yes, I do," said Alice, "but—"

"Well, if you don't care for tea," interrupted the March Hare, "you could at least make polite conversation."

"I have been trying very hard to make conversation," said Alice. "I have been trying to ask you about the White—"

"Wait! I have an idea," said the March Hare. "Let's change the subject."

Alice couldn't believe her ears.

"Tell me, why is a raven like a writing desk?" asked the Mad Hatter.

"Oh, I do like riddles," said Alice. "Let me see now. Why is a raven like a writing desk?"

"What a silly question!" said the Mad Hatter.

"But it was *your* question!" said Alice.

"Here, have a cup of tea," said the March Hare.

"Tea! Tea, indeed!" said Alice, knowing she would never get a cup of tea at this tea party. Either the March Hare would take it back or the Mad Hatter would call for clean cups and move everyone down.

"I haven't the time for this," said Alice, and she got up.

"Time? Time? Who's got the time?" asked the March Hare.
Suddenly Alice heard a familiar voice.

"No time! No time! Hello! Good-bye! I'm late. I must fly!"
said the White Rabbit, hurrying by.

"Mr. White Rabbit! Wait! I want to talk to you!" called Alice.
She started to run after him. Then she remembered her
manners.

"Thank you for the tea!" called Alice, before she realized
that she hadn't had any.

"Well, thanks for the tea *party*!" she called. And she raced
out the gate.

A SENSIBLE TALK ABOUT TEA

MAD HATTER: What do you think of that? That girl Alice joined us for tea and then just ran away.

MARCH HARE: Maybe she didn't like our tea.

MAD HATTER: Could be. But our tea is really quite good.

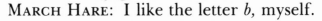

MARCH HARE: I like the letter *b*, myself.

MAD HATTER: We are not talking about the letter *t*. We are talking about tea, the drink.

MARCH HARE: Oh, you mean the kind of tea you pour boiling water over and drink with lemon or honey or milk? The tea made from specially prepared leaves?

MAD HATTER: Yes, yes, that tea. I say we should have a sensible talk about it.

MARCH HARE: Well, all right then, we will. Did you know that most of the tea we drink comes from India and China?

16

MAD HATTER: Of course I did. I even know a legend about it. It goes like this: A long, long time ago—the year 2737 B.C. to be exact—a Chinese emperor called Shen-Nung told his people to boil their water before drinking it to make sure it was clean. One day, some leaves from a hanging plant dropped into a pot of water that was boiling, and guess what—Emperor Shen-Nung discovered tea!

MARCH HARE: That's a good story about how hot tea was discovered. The story of iced tea is a good one, too. In the summer of 1904, a salesman at the St. Louis World's Fair was having trouble selling his hot tea. He decided that because the weather was so hot, people would like something cold to drink, so he poured his hot tea over ice. Everyone loved it!

17

MAD HATTER: That's not all that happened to tea in 1904. In New York City, another salesman started sending his customers samples of tea leaves in small silk bags instead of the tin containers tea usually came in. He was surprised when he found out that the people were leaving the tea in the bags and pouring water right over them. And we've used tea bags made of cloth or paper ever since!

MARCH HARE: Here's my favorite fact: After water, tea is the most popular drink in the world!

MAD HATTER: It is? Why, let's go have some. We can ask that girl, Alice, to join us. If we can find her, that is. And we'll ask her if she has any friends who would like to join us, too.

18

ALICE DECIDES TO HAVE A TEA PARTY

The Mad Hatter and the March Hare looked everywhere for Alice. But she was always just ahead of them, having this adventure and that.

Finally, when Alice decided she'd had quite enough adventures and wanted to go back where she came from, she began to run. She ran and ran. Then suddenly she was floating through space.

The next thing Alice knew, she was under the tree where she had started out. Her cat, Dinah, was curled up in her lap.

"Wake up, Alice, dear," she heard her sister say. "You've been sleeping for a long time. It's time for us to go home."

Alice had lots to think about on the way. She thought about rabbits who were always running late and about tea parties celebrating unbirthdays, where no one go   drink a drop of tea.

Then Alice got an idea. She decided to   n unbirthday tea party of her own and invite her friends. And she was going to make sure they got to drink all the tea they wanted!

THE GOOD MANNERS TEST

"Now, which friends shall I invite to my party?" Alice said to Dinah. "I certainly won't invite anyone like the White Rabbit. He'd be late, if he ever came at all. And I wouldn't invite anyone like the Mad Hatter or the March Hare, either. They would just act too silly and no one would get to drink any tea because they would be yelling, 'Clean cup! Move down!' "

No, I'm only going to invite friends who have good manners, thought Alice. But how will I know who they are? I know! I'll give them a test!

Here's Alice's Good Manners Test. See if you can pass it.

1. A friend calls and says, "I'm having a tea party next Sunday at three. Would you like to come?" What do you say?

(a) I can't. I have to give my rhinoceros a bath.

(b) Thank you. I'd love to come. Is there anything I can bring?

(c) No way. I hate tea!

2. When you get to the tea party, the food is set out on the table.
What do you do?

(a) Grab three of everything you like to eat.

(b) Dip your pinkie into the whipped cream for a taste.

(c) Wait for your hostess to say, "Please help yourself."

3. You are sitting at the table and have just taken a bite of your sandwich. You remember something you wanted to tell your friends. What do you do?

(a) Wait until you have swallowed what you are eating before you begin to speak.

(b) Jump up and down and wave your arms wildly to get everyone's attention.

(c) Speak with your mouth full of sandwich so that no one can understand you and food flies all over the room.

4. It's very late and time for you to leave the party.
What do you say?

(a) This party was terrible. I'm so sorry you made me come.

(b) I'm having a party next week, but you're not invited.

(c) Thank you for inviting me. I had a lovely time.

To find out the correct answers, turn the page upside down. Did you pass the Good Manners Test?

1. b   2. c   3. a   4. c

TALKING TEAPOT ONE: Which hand do you use to stir your tea?
TALKING TEAPOT TWO: Neither one. A spoon is best.

"Whoever passes the Good Manners Test will be invited to my party," said Alice to Dinah.

Dinah looked up and flicked her tail.

"Don't worry, dear Dinah. You don't have to take any test. You're invited to my party no matter what. Now, let's see. I'll need invitations. And I know just how to make them."

Here's how to make Alice's inviting invitations
when you host your own tea party.

Fold pieces of construction paper in half to make cards.

On another piece of colored paper draw pictures that will fit on the front of each invitation.

Try drawing the White Rabbit's pocketwatch or
a pretty teacup or teapot.

Cut out the drawings and paste them on the front
of the invitations.

You can write this poem inside or make up one
of your own:

> As you can see,
> It's time for tea.
> Please mark the date
> And don't be late!

Then add the following information:

Where: (Write your address.)

When: (Write the time and date.)

RSVP (That means please call to let me know if
you can make it!): (Write your phone number
here.)

Note: If you want to mail your invitations, paste the drawings on
the inside of the cards. Then use the front of each invitation for
the address and stamp. Tape or staple the card closed.

A TASTY TEA-PARTY MENU

"Food. I'll need food at my party," Alice said. "I can't let my guests go hungry. What shall I make?"

Here's what Alice decided to serve at her party.
You might serve the same things at your own tea party.
(Remember, you should always have a grown-up help when you cook, and teas without caffeine are best.)

MERRY BERRY TEA

Warm a teapot by rinsing it with hot water.

Place three herbal-berry tea bags and three orange slices in the pot.

Pour in boiling water and let it sit for five minutes.

Put one fresh orange slice on the rim of each cup and pour in the tea.

26

TEA SANDWICHES

Cut the crusts off slices of white bread and add
  tasty toppings, such as

  Cream cheese and sliced cucumber,

  Peanut butter and jelly,

  Butter and sugar,

  Turkey and mayonnaise.

Cut the bread into small triangles, as shown.

Place a pretty napkin or doily on a plate.

Arrange the sandwiches on the plate with slices
  of carrots and celery.

HOT APPLE CIDER

Pour one large bottle or can of apple cider into
  a pot and have a grown-up heat it up.

Place a cinnamon stick in each cup and serve.

Note: If you want to serve cold tea or cider, you can make
  berry ice cubes. The night before your party, fill an ice-
  cube tray halfway and place a blueberry or other berry
  in the center of each cube.

CINNAMON TOAST

Toast two pieces of bread for each guest.

Spread with butter.

Sprinkle lightly with cinnamon and sugar.

Cut toast into triangles.

Set out a bowl of raisins and invite your friends
to make raisin faces on their toast.

28

FRUIT SALAD

Mix sliced apples and peeled oranges and bananas
in a big bowl.
Add half a cup of grapes and half a cup of raisins.
Pour in a quarter cup of orange juice.
Add a tablespoon of honey and mix everything
together.
Serve in pretty bowls.

TOPSY-TURVY TABLE DECORATIONS

Wonderland was such a topsy-turvy place, thought Alice. So I am going to make my party table topsy-turvy, too. Now, everything's got to be just right. Or just wrong. Or just topsy-turvy!

Here's how to make a topsy-turvy table.

TABLECLOTH

Cover the table with a piece of plain paper.

Put a glass full of crayons on the table. When your guests come, they can help you decorate your "tablecloth."

NAPKIN RINGS

Cut out two-inch-high hearts from construction paper.

Write a name on each heart, but don't use the names of your friends. Think of other names, or write the same name on every napkin ring!

Glue sparkles around the names.

Make a small hole at each side of the heart and attach colored ribbons, approximately four inches long.

Tie around napkins, as shown.

30

CENTERPIECE

Cut out paper flowers like the one shown here,
or design your own.

Draw funny faces on the flowers.

Tape each flower onto a pipe cleaner.

Put clay into a pretty bowl or basket and stick
pipe-cleaner flowers into the clay.

If you have colored ribbons, tie some onto the
basket.

TABLE SETTINGS

To make your table look like it was set by the
Mad Hatter, you should make an arrange-
ment of different-colored knives, forks,
spoons, plates, and napkins. Ask your friends
to each bring a cup and saucer if they have
one. That way, nothing will match anything
else!

MAD HATTER HATS

"I would invite the Mad Hatter to my party," said Alice, "but I don't think he could pass the Good Manners Test. But wait. I know what we can do instead. We can make hats in his honor. I think he would like that, don't you, Dinah?"

"Meow!" said Dinah. She thought the Mad Hatter would like that very well.

Here's how to make Mad Hatter Hats.

WHAT YOU WILL NEED
Paper plates.
Ribbon or string.
Lots of good things for trimming the hats—crepe paper, foil, yarn, egg cartons, construction paper, glitter, macaroni. (Ask your guests to bring things for trimming, too.)

WHAT TO DO

Make a hole with a hole puncher on each side of
    each plate.

Cut two lengths of ribbon or string (about two
    feet long) for each plate.

Push one ribbon through each hole.

Tie a knot at the top of each ribbon to keep it
    from coming out of the hole.

Now the hats are ready for trimming.

If you want to make a tall hat, roll construction
    paper the long way and glue or staple it to-
    gether.

Cut four slits at the bottom and fold out as shown.

Glue or staple the construction paper to the plate.

TEA-PARTY GAMES

"What would a party be without games?" said Alice. "It wouldn't be much fun at all. We must have lots of games!"

Here are some games
Alice plans to play at her party.
You can play them at your party, too.

MUSICAL TEA PARTY

"Clean cup! Move down!" called the Mad Hatter and the March Hare at their tea party. Alice had not even touched her cup of tea, but she had to change her seat anyway. The party turned into a game of musical chairs.

HOW TO PLAY THE GAME

Have one less chair around the table than the number of players.

All the players walk around the chairs while a radio or a tape plays music.

A grown-up who is standing with his or her back to the players turns off the music.

When the music stops, each player must hurry to a seat.

Whoever is left standing is out of the game.

Take away a chair and repeat until there is just one player sitting in one chair. That player wins.

WHERE DO I GO? WHAT DO I DO?

When Alice was trying to find her way through Wonderland, she came to a tree with signs pointing in all different directions. Alice was very confused. Here's a game that's not quite so confusing. It's just very silly!

HOW TO MAKE THE GAME

Draw direction signs, as shown.

Write instructions like the following on each line:

> Take three baby steps backward.
>
> Jump up and down while you whistle your favorite song.
>
> Take one giant step to the right.
>
> Try to touch your elbows to your ears.
>
> Twirl to the left two times.
>
> Shake hands with everyone at the party and say, "How do you do?"

Tape the signs to a wall.

HOW TO PLAY THE GAME

One player at a time is blindfolded and pointed in the direction of the signs. When the player touches a sign, he or she removes the blindfold and follows the directions.

I FOUND THE RABBITS!

Alice went through Wonderland trying to catch the White Rabbit. Here is a game in which your friends must catch ten white rabbits!

HOW TO PLAY THE GAME

Before your guests come, trace ten rabbits, as shown, on white paper. Then cut them out.

Have a separate piece of paper for each player with the numbers 1 through 10 written on it.

When all your guests have arrived, wait with them in one room while a grown-up hides the rabbits around the rest of the house.

Give each player a pencil and a piece of paper with the numbers on it.

When a player finds a rabbit, he or she crosses out a number.

The first player to cross out all the numbers calls out, "I found the rabbits!" and shows everyone where the ten rabbits were hidden.

MOUSE, MOUSE, DORMOUSE!

Alice never knew when the Dormouse would pop up from inside a teapot or when he would come sailing down from the sky. He was a funny little mouse, indeed!

HOW TO PLAY THE GAME

This game is played the same way as "Duck, Duck, Goose."

The players sit in a circle.

One player who is "It" walks around the outside of the circle and taps each player lightly on the head. With each tap, he or she says, "Mouse."

Finally the player who is "It" taps someone and says, "Dormouse!"

The player who was tagged "Dormouse" jumps up and chases the player who is "It" around the outside of the circle.

The "Dormouse" must tag "It" before "It" sits down.

If the "Dormouse" catches and tags "It," then that player is still "It."

If "It" sits down first, the "Dormouse" becomes "It."

RHYME TIME

Poems are fun, thought Alice. I just love the one the Dormouse made up. Why, I think I'll share some poems at my party.

THE LAST WORD
Here are some of the poems Alice heard in Wonderland. One player reads a poem, and the others call out an ending. It doesn't have to be the right ending, it just has to rhyme.

I'm late! I'm late!
For a very important _____.
(date)

Twinkle, twinkle, little bat
How I wonder what you're at.
Up above the world you fly
Like a tea tray in the _____.
(sky)

How doth the little crocodile
Improve his shining tail,
And pour the waters of the Nile
On every golden _____!
(scale)

40

THE UNBIRTHDAY SONG

Words and Music by Mack David, Al Hoffman, and Jerry Livingston.

We must be sure to sing "The Unbirthday Song," thought Alice. I'll hand out the words to all my guests.

A very merry unbirthday to us, to us
If there are no objections, let it be unanimous
Oh, a very merry unbirthday
A very merry unbirthday
A very merry unbirthday to us.

A . . . a . . . a . . . a . . . a very merry unbirthday to me
To who?
To me!
Oh, you!
A very merry unbirthday to you
Who me?
Yes you!
Oh, me!
Let's all congratulate us with
Another cup of tea
A very merry unbirthday to youououou!

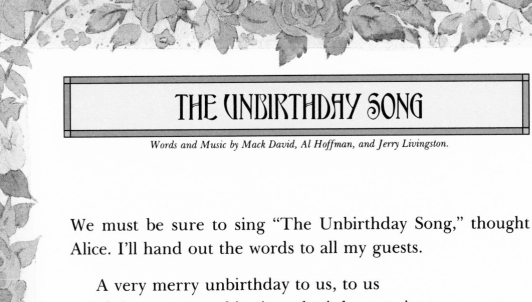

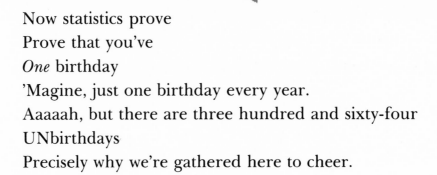

Now statistics prove
Prove that you've
One birthday
'Magine, just one birthday every year.
Aaaaah, but there are three hundred and sixty-four
UNbirthdays
Precisely why we're gathered here to cheer.

A very merry unbirthday—to me?
To you!
A very merry unbirthday—for me?
For you!
Now blow the candle out, my dear
And make your wish come true
A very merry unbirthday to you.

"I can't let my friends leave without knowing their fortunes. The best way to tell a fortune is by reading tea leaves, but I don't know how to. Do you, Dinah?" asked Alice.

Dinah just yawned.

"There won't be tea leaves in the cups anyway, because I'm using tea bags. But wait! I know what to do," said Alice.

Here's Alice's idea for telling fortunes. You can do it, too.

Trace the leaf below enough times to have one for each guest and write a fortune on each one.

Cut out and fold the leaves so the fortunes are hidden. Put them into a jar.

Have your friends close their eyes and take turns picking fortunes.

Here are some of the things you can write:

Somebody likes you.

You will get new shoes.

The man in the moon will smile at you.

You are going to be invited to a birthday party.

The teacher will ask you a hard question tomorrow.

You are smart.

You will meet a funny white rabbit and follow him down the rabbit hole!

43

AFTER THE PARTY

"That was quite a nice tea party, if I do say so myself," said Alice.

"Meow!" agreed Dinah.

"Our guests had very good manners. They all got to drink as much tea as they wanted. They made lots of funny hats. And . . . and . . . ahhh," yawned Alice. "I'm feeling awfully sleepy."

Alice curled up in a chair. As soon as she got comfortable, Dinah jumped into her lap.

Alice looked around the room. "I must clean up this mess, but that can wait till later, don't you think?" asked Alice.

But Dinah didn't answer. She was sleeping.

So Alice closed her eyes, and in no time she was asleep, too. Soon she was dreaming. Was she dreaming about magic mushrooms and talking flowers? Well, what do you think?